REVIEWED
JUN 2021

D0527556

Martin Boroson is director of the Temenos Project,
an organisation that encourages the visionary potential
of art and artists. A graduate in philosophy from Yale University,
he earned an MBA from the Yale School of Management
and trained in transpersonal psychology with Dr. Stanislav Grof.
In his lectures and workshops, he expands on the themes
of Becoming Me, teaching core spiritual ideas
in a practical, modern way.

Christopher Gilvan-Cartwright graduated from St Martin's
School of Art and then completed a postgraduate degree
in Fine Art Painting at the Krakow Academy of Fine Art in Poland.
He has won various awards and scholarships, including the British
Council/Polish Government Travel Scholarship and the Royal Overseas
League Travel Bursary, with which he travelled to India and Nepal.
His work has been exhibited extensively in Europe.

EAST RIDING
OF YORKSHIRE COUNCIL
Schools Library Service

PROJECT
September 2011

For Andrew and Tobs with love ★ M.B.

For Isobel with love ★ C.G-C.

EAST RIDING OF
YORKSHIRE SLS
901569870
Bertrams   03/03/2011
231   £6.99

Becoming Me: A Story of Creation copyright © Frances Lincoln Limited 2000
Text copyright © Martin Boroson 2000
Illustrations copyright © Christopher Gilvan-Cartwright 2000

First published in Great Britain in 2000 by
Frances Lincoln Children's Books, 4 Torriano Mews,
Torriano Avenue, London NW5 2RZ
www.franceslincoln.com

First paperback edition 2002

All rights reserved

No part of this publication may be reproduced, stored in a retrieval system, or transmitted,
in any form, or by any means, electrical, mechanical, photocopying, recording or otherwise
without the prior written permission of the publisher or a licence permitting restricted copying.
In the United Kingdom such licences are issued by the Copyright Licensing Agency,
Saffron House, 6-10 Kirby Street, London EC1N 8TS.

British Library Cataloguing in Publication Data available on request

ISBN 978-0-7112-1834-5

Designed by Sarah Slack

Set in Voodoo and Meta

Printed in Dongguan, Guangdong, China by Kwong Fat Offset Printing in December 2010

9 8 7 6 5 4

becoming
me

a story of creation

written by martin boroson

illustrated by christopher gilvan-cartwright

F

FRANCES LINCOLN
CHILDREN'S BOOKS

Once upon
a time ...

I was.

There was nobody who knew that I was ...

But I was.

I liked to make myself into different shapes.
Lots of different shapes – all me.
Everywhere I looked there was only me.
I must be **very big.**

I played by myself for ages.
It seemed like forever.
Then I started to get lonely.
I wanted someone else to play with,
someone who wasn't ME.

So I took a deep breath,
gathered all my strength together,
and squeezed really hard.
I started to feel dizzy.
It felt like I was falling.

And then suddenly, in a big burst,

I became ...

something ELSE!

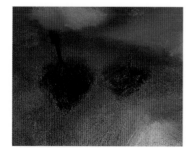 This was so much fun,
I did it again and again,
lots of different ways.
I do it all the time now.

I can become all kinds of things,
things that ...

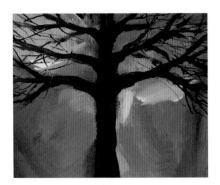

grow

and swim

and fly

and crawl

and run.

One day, I squeezed extra hard.
I pushed and I pushed and I
pushed, and then all of a sudden,
I became ...

YOU.

What is this thing I'm in?
Just one moment ago I was SO BIG
and now I'm SO little.
It's like I'm all wrapped up in love.

But as soon as I become you,
you forget that you're me.

In time, you forget all about me.

Every so often, you wonder who you are.
And I'm right here, reminding you.

I'm always busy now, cheering you on.

I like it best when you discover me.
Then we play together, you and I.

And sometimes you realize
that you **are** me.

Sometimes you forget that everything else is me too.

But even
then ...

I still love you ...

little ME.

ACKNOWLEDGEMENTS

I am grateful to Stan and Christina Grof, and to my many friends, colleagues, teachers and clients who have been inspired by their extraordinary work. More than any others, Barbara Dickey, Martin Duffy, Barbara Egan, Anne Fitzmaurice, and Nienke Merbis helped at the long birth of this story in me, and I am deeply grateful for their love, friendship and patience.

In refining my ideas for this story, I benefited from the research and writing of several leading consciousness researchers. Of particular help were: *The Cosmic Game* and *The Holotropic Mind* by Stanislav Grof; *A Brief History of Everything* and *Sex, Ecology, Spirituality* by Ken Wilber; and *The Creative Cosmos* by Ervin Laszlo. I am indebted to the ground-breaking, integral vision presented in these works.

For their invaluable editorial and production advice, constant support and love, thank you to: Barbara Boroson, Florence Boroson, Louis Boroson, Andrew Dodd and Joe Rutt.

I feel blessed to have found the publishing team at Frances Lincoln, particularly Kate Cave, Sarah Slack, and especially Cathy Fischgrund, whose big heart and wide eyes opened to this story immediately, and whose sharp mind steered its course to publication. It has been wonderful working with them.

M.B.

To find out more about the ideas in this book, visit the website at:
www.becomingme.com

MORE TITLES FROM
FRANCES LINCOLN CHILDREN'S BOOKS

A Ladder to the Stars
Simon Puttock
Illustrated by Alison Jay

A little girl looks up to the sky and makes a wish to climb so
high she can dance with the stars. One star hears her wish,
and decides to make her dream come true. A wonderful,
timeless tale full of fantasy and hope.

The Star-Bearer
A Creation Myth from Ancient Egypt
Dianne Hofmeyr
Illustrated by Jude Daly

When the godchild Atum emerges from inky silence to
begin his work of creation, at first all goes well: from his breath
and hands come the playful gods of air and rain, followed by
Geb, god of the earth, and Nut, goddess of the sky.
But then things start to go wrong...

Lord of the Animals
A Native American Creation Myth
Fiona French

Coyote has created the world and its creatures, and now he
gathers a council to decide how they will make the being who will
rule over them all. Fiona French's boldly illustrated retelling of a
Native American Miwok myth gives an intriguing explanation
of how human beings began.

Frances Lincoln titles are available from all good bookshops.
You can also buy books and find out more about your favourite titles,
authors and illustrators on our website: www.franceslincoln.com